Hiclecopotamus

Geeta Dharmarajan
Art by Atanu Roy

ॐKATHA

One day, in the middle of the afternoon, a most enormous thing fell into the White Lily Pond in Guimohar Jungle.

CRASH! ...

CLATTER! ...

Help!

Muyal the Rabbit,
Hanu the Monkey,
Popat the Parrot
screamed ...

Everyone was so busy being afraid that they didn't see the 'thing' carefully walk out of the pond. Muyal was the first to spot him.

Hey, you there! Who are you?

Muyal asked boldly, though her voice came out rather squeaky.

After all, the 'thing' was so BIG!

HiC!

I am Hawasi,
a hi–hic!–copo–tamus.

The strange animal
said, giving a tiny
little hiccup.

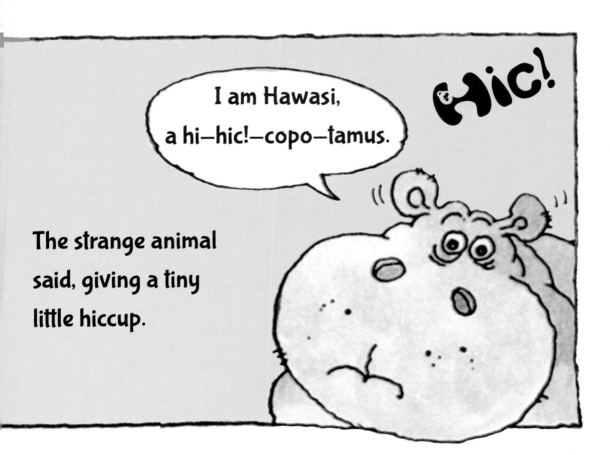

At once, Hawasi broke into tears.

"I wan ... t to go—hic—home!" he
wailed, bouncing up a foot or two.

Hic!

BWAAA!

But how did you get here?

Ela the Caterpillar asked.

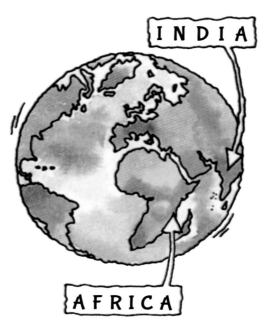

INDIA

AFRICA

I was with my Ma. Suddenly I got the hiccups and—hic—sw...ish! I went into the air!

My Ma couldn't stop me. My aunts couldn't stop me. Even my strong Papa couldn't!

And here I am! I am scared of getting another huge hiccup like that! I might fly off and not come down at all!

Hawasi said, looking at the animals around him.

"We'll help you get rid of your hiccups!" said Muyal helpfully.

"And get me back home?" asked Hawasi hopefully.

"Sure. We'll try," said Hanu. "Let's call our other friends too! Someone might come up with a good cure for hiccups!"

So off went Muyal to call the haathi-log, the tigers and the bats and the spiders. And everyone.

Soon they were all busy thinking.

"Water!" said Forest Fox suddenly.
"That's what we foxes drink when we
hiccup. It works every time!"

"Thanks!" said Hawasi,
"Water I love!"

He promptly stepped
into the White Lily
Pond ... and just
disappeared.

Just then ...

Listen! If we get rid of his hiccups, how will we get him back home?

"Oh no!" groaned Hanu when he heard Tejas the Tiger. "We never thought of that!"

"What we really need is a way to give him a huge hiccup that'll take him all the way back home, the same way he came!" said Popat the Parrot.

"We'll tickle him!" said the ants.

"We'll tell him such crazy jokes that they'll take him all the way home!" said the monkeys. "Goody!" shouted Hawasi, his small eyes twinkling. "Here I come Mama!"

The ants tickled Hawasi.

And everyone shouted all the jokes and the funny riddles they knew.

Where does a seven-foot gorilla sleep?

Anywhere he wants to!

Why does a stork stand on one leg?

Because if she lifted the other one up too, she'd fall down!

What is as big as a hippo, but weighs nothing?

A hippo's shadow!

Where do frogs keep their money?

In river banks!

Monkeys, elephants, caterpillars and birds were all giggling their heads off!

In their middle was Hawasi, roaring with laughter. He'd never heard so many jokes before!

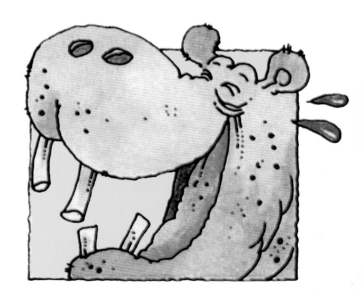

And right in the middle of a crazy elephant joke, Hawasi hiccuped!

A really huge, hippo-sized

Hic!

Up he went flying, right over the banyan tree, the way he'd come.

"Bye! And thanks!" shouted Hawasi from the sky as he flew off happily.

"Bye, bye! Happy landing!" called out all the animals.

BACK HOME!

And, oh yes, before I forget. Only yesterday the animals of Gulmohar Jungle heard a big 'thank you!' grunt from Mzima Springs, Africa.

Yes, you guessed right! It was Hawasi the Hiccopotamus!

Guess who?

Its name means 'river horse'. It looks like a pig. It's very big, fat and heavy (it weighs as much as you and more than 200 others like you put together!), but it can run faster than you can and can swim beautifully.

Have you guessed its name? It's

HIPPOPOTAMUS,

of course!

The skin on the hippo's back and sides is as thick as the width of your four fingers, and so it's not afraid of any other creature, except a full-grown lion maybe.

The hippo's mouth is so huge that you could easily step into it—not that you'd ever want to! Hippos are usually peaceful and friendly animals, if you leave them alone. But an angry hippo can crush a boat with its jaws!

Hippos love resting in their African rivers all day long. Sometimes they take underwater walks on the riverbed, gathering huge mouthfuls of weeds and water plants (hippos are vegetarian). They have special flaps of skin that cover their nostrils to stop the water from going into their lungs.

Baby hippos are born underwater and can swim even before they can walk! Only one baby is born at a time. As soon as a baby learns to walk, she or he likes to go off on adventures of her or his own. But mother hippos nudge their babies back gently. Baby hippos learn by watching their mothers—to stay out of danger, to find food, and to have fun!

Geeta Dharmarajan loves writing stories for children. She was one of the editors of *Target,* a magazine for children, and *The Pennsylvania Gazette*, the magazine of the University of Pennsylvania. She has been awarded the prestigious Padma Shri in 2012 for her distinguished service in the fields of literature and education.

With over 100 children's books under his belt, **Atanu Roy** has devoted much of his creative prowess to children's literature. Roy's use of bold colours and vivid details, capture the hearts and eyes of his readers. It's no surprise then that Roy, who once worked as a political cartoonist for *India Today*, has won awards like the Children's Choice Award for Book Illustrations and the IBBY Certificate of Honour for Illustrations. His studio is located in Gurgaon.

KATHA

First published in *Tamasha!* in 1991
Copyright © Katha, 2014
Text copyright © Geeta Dharmarajan, 1991
Illustrations copyright © Atanu Roy, 1991
All rights reserved. No part of this book may be reproduced or utilized in any form without the prior written permission of the publisher.
Printed in New Delhi
ISBN 978-93-82454-24-3

KATHA is a registered nonprofit organization devoted to enhancing the joys of reading amongst children and adults. Katha Schools are situated in the slums and streets of Delhi and tribal villages of Arunachal Pradesh.
A3 Sarvodaya Enclave, Sri Aurobindo Marg
New Delhi 110 017
Phone: 4141 6600 . 4182 9998 . 2652 1752
Fax: 2651 4373
E-mail: marketing@katha.org, Website: www.katha.org

Ten per cent of sales proceeds from this book will support the quality education of children studying in Katha Schools. Katha regularly plants trees to replace the wood used in the making of its books.

First Reprint 2015, Second Reprint 2016, Third Reprint 2017